The Storyteller

by

Eddie J Martin

I0538571

There's nothing like sitting by a cozy fireplace, glass of wine and a good book... Enter the storyteller.

Acknowledgement:

Carvin and Marilyn Stone.
The years seem to just fly by I'm glad you 2 have been there.

Imogene Martin Bird,
but for you there'd be no Ruben Kane, Willow or Dumas; thanks for everything you've done.

James Collier
Years pass but that one year (1964) will always stay in memory.

Mary and Herbert Lee, You Beautiful people.

Ms. Thang is missing

Chapter 1

Hello, miss Thelma this is miss Ada, Wilma's mother, have you seen her? she left home a couple hours ago and haven't been back since she only went down to the store to pick up a loaf of bread and milk and I haven't seen her since did she happen to stop over there?

No, I'm afraid I haven't seen her, and my kids have been at the house all day I'll ask them if they've seen her but I'm sure she'll be home soon. I hope you find her. She's the one they call Miss Thing, isn't she?

Yes, she is, the kids call her that.

Thank you miss Thelma would you keep an eye open for her.

Have you checked with the other kids in the neighborhood miss ada? If you can't find her you may have to call the police.

You are my first call miss Thelma, but I'll be calling everyone else I can think of. The police may be next.

Your daughter is only seven years old, isn't she? Kind of young for you to let her go to the store alone.

Tell me about it, Ada said.

After driving around the neighborhood she decided to go to her girlfriends house sometimes Wilma will go over there. Once there she heard Georgia and her old man going at it as they usually do that was one of the reasons, she warned Wilma about going there. she knocked on the door and Georgia old man open it and look like he was in no mood to talk to anyone she asked him Has Wilma been there and he said that no, the little ***** hasn't been over here. Right away that made her angry, Georgia came to the door nose bleeding, he grabbed her by the hair and threw her back on the floor and she just couldn't control herself and jumped on Georges back and commits to beat him. Georgia got off the floor and they both started beating him with everything that was round the house at that point he ran out the house and down the street bleeding like a pig. Ada helped Georgia clean herself up and she swore that he wooden come back after that beating, they gave him. Ada commenced to tell her why she was there, and Georgia ask her why she didn't call her ex-husband or the police?

Well, you know why I didn't call the police and my ex-husband is really out the question. She had told Georgia long ago how they acquired her daughter. She couldn't have kids so one day her X came home with a newborn baby girl where she came from, she didn't know, she figured later on that her ex had stolen the baby from some hospital and that was some six years ago the only one she ever talked to about that was Georgia so police were out the question. But if it comes down to it, she will have to call Jason her x. Any ideas she asked Georgia?

The only thing I know is to start beating the bushes Wilma is a beautiful little girl and you know they have the weirdos out there that would love to have her so let's go.

A few miles down the road they saw Georgia's X and he didn't look to swell they passed him by and Just shook their head made her feel good and say, "glad I never married that fool."

They searched the town over and asked everyone they knew but no one had seen Wilma so finally Ada bit the bullet and call Jason.

******

I knew you couldn't take care of that girl said Jason you give her too much leeway for a little girl now you'll listen to me want you.

I didn't ask you all that Jason all I want to know is have you seen her, is she over there?

No and no but I guess I'll have to get out here and search for her myself.

C hapter 2

who was that Jason?

My ex-Jason said. Wilma had gone missing again and she don't know where she's at. That's the second or third time that little girl has gone missing she knows she's too young to let her go just about anywhere she wants to go.

What about calling the police Raiman said?

You know how I feel about that, I told you how all that came about. Ada thanks I stole the girl from some hospital and I never told her any different but what really happened is that some young girl had the baby in an alley, and I spotted her sense ada was trying to have a baby and never could I convinced the girl to give the baby to me I think she was going to put her in the trash anyway. So, I just let ada keep on thinking that I stole her. Now I have to get out here and search for her I like that little girl and I wouldn't want anything to happen to her.

Do you need any help Raiman asked?

If I do, I'll let you know Jason said.

Two years after Jason found the baby, he and ada separated it seems as though Jason liked men more than he did women more than her anyway, but they stayed friends and Wilma kept them more than friends they made an agreement that he could see her anytime he wanted and that he would help with her upbringing, so far things had worked out fairly good except for the fact that ada thought Wilma was more grown than she wanted Jason didn't like that after all she was only six years old.

Jason got dressed kissed Raiman and left the house, where would be a good place to start looking for her? If she's been apprehended there is no telling where she could be. The police station I'll go there and see if I can BS them.

At the police station he went to the lost and found and asked if they had any kids missing or had found any kids live or dead? They told him that they had a couple young kids that they found dead, but they didn't know who they were was he missing anyone? One of my neighbors is missing her daughter and maybe I thought I would help her search could he take a look at the kids? He was taking down to the morgue and looked at the bodies one was a young boy of about 9 years old and the other was a girl of about 8 but neither one of them was Wilma. What is this girl name that you are looking for the officer asked him? They call her Ms. Thang Jason said her name is Wilma George, but these two are not her.

The officer took Ms. Things vitals and said they would keep it on records in case she was to come in. Jason thanks him and said it is not too often he runs into an officer that gave up that kind of information; must be some kind of public relation thing. At least it's more than ada would have done she's probably still afraid that he'd stolen her.

C hapter 3

Georgia's X had spotted her an Ada pass by and thought now was a good time to go back to the house and get his things which he did. While he was there, he went through the house and took the money that she had hidden an everything else he could find that he could put in his pocket. He wouldn't be coming back there anymore he was tired of her anyway and that crazy friend of hers, ada, he never did like her.

Back on the block he met up with J-rod and jelly they were moving out of their apartment out of town they still had two weeks left on their rental agreement and decided that he could stay there just pick up the payments. He agreed with that they didn't even want any money up front. As he was helping them put a few things in the car he notices a little girl in the back seat it was Wilma. Isn't that Miss Thing he asked her mother has been looking for her all over town. I'll tell you what Jelly said you just keep your mouth **** about seeing her can you do that? Sure, I can do that but what do you plan on doing with her?

They've got people in Oklahoma that's looking for a little girl and willing to pay good money for her, so we are going to take her out there and collect on that money. You know that's kidnapping don't you I hope you know that. You just keep your mouth shut and everything will be alright. OK but I hope you know that Jason punk will be looking for her. We not worried about that Gerard we on our way out of town right now, so we won't be seeing you again and if you happen to run into Ms. Thang's people just keep your mouth close.

Gerald moved into the apartment and decided to go down to the pool hall on the way there he ran into Jason they had been knowing each other for some years he liked Jason but didn't like Ada once he started going with Ada, they kind of lost contact with each other. I wonder if she ever found out that Jason was Homosexual? Jason informed him that he was searching for miss thang had he seen her? Gerald thought for a minute wondering whether he should say anything or not after all he was closer to Jason then he was to j-rod and Jelly. as far as miss thing he could take her or leave her, he wasn't too much of a kid person anyway.

No man, I haven't seen her but look, look up j-rod and Jelly they see everything in the neighborhood and I'm sure they may have run across her or maybe not, check them out. I appreciate that Gerald you a good friend I'll start looking for j-rad and Jelly right now.

Eventually Jason stops by the Sinclair service station to get gas an happened to mention that he was looking for miss thang and that he heard that j-rod and Jelly knew where she was. The service attendant told Jason that they stop by there a few hours ago to get gas and were headed out of town, he wasn't sure, but he thought he saw a little girl in the back seat he wasn't sure though. You got to be ******** me Jason said. They wouldn't have just taken miss thang and abducted her, would they? I don't know the attendant said maybe I'm wrong about seeing Ms. thang, but it sure did look like her. It was a little girl I'm sure.

I be damn, Gerard knew J-rod and Jelly had miss thang but didn't say so he probably knew where they were going, Gerard will tell him if they had Ms. Thang or his *** is mine and that's a fact.

Chapter 4

By this time ada had taken Georgia back home with no luck on finding miss thing she did receive a call from Jason, and he told her what he learned about J-rod and Jelly having her, from what he had heard they were taking her out of town to sell her and he was following. She told Jason that she wanted to go along but he said no, absolutely not.

He also called Raiman and told him the situation and Raiman asked him did he need him to go along Jason again said no if he need help, he'll call him.

Oklahoma, that's a long way maybe he'll have some luck along the way after all they do need to sleep and miss thang will surely be slowing them down. He thought to himself what type of weapons he had, and he thought about the shotgun that was in the trunk with a hunting knife, also a derringer that was in the glove compartment that held two shots and he thought he had extra bullets for it. It would have to do. Next time he stopped he would have to check it all.

J-rod and Jelly were two bad boys they always have been into something from stealing stuff from the gas station and from stores an everything you could think of they were into it so I guess now there into Abducting little girls, but they should have known that this little girl was his and that he would be coming after them. Jelly has people in Oklahoma maybe that's why they're going there but it really won't save them he'll be coming after them and when he catches up with them it won't be anything nice if they've harmed Ms. Thang ... he didn't want to thank about that.

On Thursday, I'm hungry, I'm hot, miss thang said. J-rod look at Jelly and said didn't we just feed this little girl a few hours ago what the hell do she want now. Jelly looked back at miss thang and saw that she was sweating she shouldn't be sweating what the hell is wrong with her now? He reached over and felt her head and told j-rod that she was burning up. You see that j-rod said there's always something goes wrong with a little kid when we took her, I told you that was a wrong move but no you just had to have this big money.

When are you taking me home to my momma, you said you would I haven't seen my Mama yet? Lay back down and go to sleep we'll stop somewhere and get you something to eat real soon.

Water, do you have any water you can give me?

Hell, no we don't have water go to sleep. What she thinks this is a gas station? And we'll be taking you home to your Mama real soon don't you fret about that.

In the next few hours J-rod and Jelly stopped at a service station went into to get something to eat and left miss thang in the car with the windows closed and the doors locked. 45 minutes later they came out got their gas and had miss thang something to eat with a drink, when they pulled out Jelly look around in the back to give Ms. Thang her food and drink and try to wake her up but couldn't. He looked at j-rod and said this girl won't wake up you better pull over to the side and see what the hell is wrong with her. J rod pulled over to the side of the road and they looked at miss thang and saw that she was sweating previously, and she wouldn't wake up. They looked at each other and knew right then that miss thang was dead and then they really freaked out. What should we do now j-rod said?

 Damn if I know Jelly said but we can't be caught with her, that's a hanging offence. We have to find someplace to Bury her and I mean quick.

J-rod and Jelly found a back Rd and they turn down it and found it was very desolate and decided that was a good place to ditch miss thang they didn't even take time to bury her just threw her out amongst the weeds and left out of there.

C hapter 5

The next day a couple of Quail hunters found the body of miss Thang and call the law, the body was taken into town and was having an autopsy when Jason happened to come into town and stopped at the service station and heard the talk about a young girl being found abandon in the woods, she was dead. His head perked up when he heard that, and he wanted to know where the body was and found out that it was in the corners office and headed there as quick as he could. Once there he informed the Officials who he was and asked to see the body.

They didn't know how she died because there were no marks on the body, and she had only been in the Woods less than 24 hours the best conclusion they could come up with was heat exhaustion and that she died of thirst.

Thirst Jason said how in the hell do you let a young kid die of thirst? Then the sheriff looks at him and said he thought Jason knew more than he was admitting. Then Jason went on to tell him the story of the abduction back in his hometown and believed it was J- Rod and Jelly who had her.

You think they had something to do with her killing the Sheriff said? I do believe that Sheriff and that's why I'll stay after them even knowing that she's dead they will have to pay. You can't just go out and take the law into your own hands that's murder the Sheriff said. You should let us take care of it.

I guess it all depends on who finds them first don't it Sheriff? Thing about it Sheriff is that you won't be able to convict me until the deed is done. They were headed to Oklahoma and that's where I'm going, would you take care of my little girl I'll be back to settle up on my way back through?

Jason called ada and told her what he found and that miss thang was dead. she didn't say anything for a long while and Then she asked had he seen the body, are you sure it was her? He said he was. he told her he was continuing on to Oklahoma, all she said was OK and thanks for calling.

Jason knew that he would never be the same until he caught up with j- rod and Jelly and put them where they belong also ada would never forgive him if he just let it go. Next stop Oklahoma City.

Meanwhile outside oh Oklahoma City J-rod and Jelly stopped at a service station slash restaurant to get something to eat and gas up, they were in there a man and a woman came in right behind them and told the cashier that this was a holdup and to give up all their money, they both had weapons in their hands and look like they were willing to use them. J-rod turned around and pull his weapon and shot the woman in the chest and the man robber shot Jelly killing him instantly. The man that was in the robbery also shot j -rod and J-rod shot him both men were killed on the spot.

C hapter 6

That next day Jason pulls into that same service station the talk of the establishment was all about the robbery and shootout. The first two men coming in, customers it was thought, the two people come in behind them one was a woman was there to Rob the place. The first two men started ordering when the second 2 pull their weapons out. The first 2 pulled their weapons out and they started firing at each other all four was killed doing the shooting. Jason had a good idea that two of the men were J-rod and Jelly.

To make sure, again he was at the corners office checking out the bodies; what to do next? Who is there to kill now? What do I do now he thought? I want to kill somebody but there is no body left to kill.

While in the corners office Jason noticed J- rods belongings on a desk and he just glanced at it noticed a note giving an address In Oklahoma City and he thought that they could have been taking Ms. Thang to be sold and he was wondering whether or not this could be the place they were taking her, if so, then maybe there will still be someone out there to kill. For Ms. Thing for Ada and for his self it would have to be done.

221 Pearl St, on the northwest side of town. Two story brick home two car garage whoever lived here wasn't doing too bad. He had made up his mind the story he would talk about meeting j-rod over there maybe that could work If not he would just wing it. A very tall dark skin girl came to the door a little heavy for my liking but one you wouldn't throw out of bed. He told her he was to meet j -rod there has he gotten in yet? the girl told him, no but

she knew how to contact someone that would put him in contact with j-rod. She invited him in the house, and he took a seat and was offered a cocktail, after 20 minutes or so she told him that someone would be over to pick him up. The person that stopped by Anne was to pick him up was a short stocky light skin fellow look like he was Creole. He told him to leave his car where it was, and they would pick it up later. After about a 45-minute drive they came to a farmhouse on the outskirts of town once in there was at least four guys in there and two girls and they welcome him just before they started beaten on his ***.

Who are you and what are you doing here one of the fellows said? Did you not know we was aware of what happened to j -rod? We don't know what happened to the little girl that he had but we know j rod is dead so who would you be, and they continued to beat on him until he let it out who he was and what he was doing down there. Before he passed out all the way he saw some people come in the back way that were handcuffed and wearing shabby clothes look like they were aliens from Mexico or Guatemala places like that he had just came upon a Human slave house, how could that have happened?

C hapter 7

Jason woke up with a bright light shining in his eyes and Raiman his boyfriend looking down at him.

How long have I been here he asked?

They picked you up three days ago and you're not in the best of health Raiman said. You had our address in your wallet the hospital calls me and I took the first plane down here. You see you needed me after all.

Jason went on to tell Raiman what had happened to him and that he had ran into a slave house he also told him where the car was if it's still there. The police were also there with Raiman taking notes an ask Jason do he think he could find the house again? You know I'm new to the town and I probably couldn't find it, but I do have the address where my car is. After a few moments of talking Jason fell back into a coma.

Raiman was notified by the police that they had found Jason's car in a parking lot at the city's park it looked like there were no damage. Raiman went through the car and found the derringer still in the glove compartment and the shotgun hidden in the trunk.

Since there was nothing for him to do so he drove around town based on the information that Jason gave him what else was he to do. The farmhouse was out of town so he concentrated on going out of town finding all the back roads he could find. That night Luck, it had to be nothing but luck for him to find that farmhouse. He parked in an area a block away and walked back and hide behind some Bush's and watch. They had at least 10 people in the truck and they were in all kinds of shape and look like all of them could use a shower, men, and women. He could go down the road a bit and call the cops but on the other hand maybe not.

C hapter 8

He never heard the young girl come up behind him and put a knife in his back and asked him "fine what you looking for"? There was nothing to say so he said nothing he came around to his right side reaching for the knife and knock it out the girls hand with his left he hit her in the stomach after she fell to the ground, he stomped her with his #12 shoes. This kind of business you can't take any chances, so he didn't. His training in the military had him well prepared for events such as these and to tell the truth he kind of missed it. It seemed like that's all she had was a knife she didn't look to well-dressed so she could have been one of the people on the truck in that case he might have made a booboo.

Half the people in the farmhouse left leaving only a few and a couple of guards so he figured what the hell he'll take the chance and he did. The shotgun in the car and a derringer was all he had but he noticed a couple of weapons that they had with any luck he would take there's. One of the men came out the back door for one reason or another and that's when he had a chance to overcome him and take his weapon. He walked in the back door while the other man was having a beer and watching TV, the other captives were in a locked room. Raiman didn't play when he walked in, he shot the man in the leg and toke his weapons and headed directly to the locked room. There were five captives in the room, and he freed them all and told them to head for the 2nd truck and the police station where they would be free. The man on the floor were moaning about his wounds and Raiman told him to shut up he could have been shot in his head. After the captives had left Raiman left his self.

Chapter 9

On the way from the farmhouse, he passed a number of police cars with their sirens going an lights on headed for the farmhouse he guessed. If they were any kind of cops at all they would find out where the other victims had been taken, not his problem now. He would go to the hospital pick up Jason and they would both head back home. Jason would have to tell ada about what happened to Ms. Thang If he havens already told her, he wouldn't want to be around for that.

That next day Raiman made it to the hospital to see Jason he went to the fifth floor and to Jason's room and found that the room was empty and new sheets was on the bed, he asked one of the nurses what happened to his friend had he been moved to another room, discharged or what? The nurse told him that she was sorry, but his friend had died in the middle of the night. Raiman was shocked and almost passed out and had to sit down, the nurse said it again that she was sorry, and would he like to speak to the doctor?

Raiman Stayed around town for a few days planning for Jason funeral he also called Ada and informed her that Jason was dead. After that he was wondering what to do with his self and thought that there was no reason in going back home because there was nothing left back there for him so where to go? He'd always like and heard of Nevada so why not go there After all Nevada is right next door to California.

End

Remember when.

"Joe", "Joe", come quick my grandmother screamed for my grand-dad, and bring the gun. She had come out the back door and spotted me jumping back and forth over a large snake, you remember the way we used to do with just a crack in the sidewalk, But I have to say he was stretched out length wise. I was about 4 or 5 years old at the time. Anyway, she got me away from the snake and he went underneath the house and we never saw him again but there were things like chickens and pigs gone missing from time to time as I remember I never did go underneath that house after that when I think back now, I know why.

It's a wonder how the mind can think back to times like that when you were a young kid from time to time a memory will come up like that it happens to me all the time. I'm really not that smart never did that good in school so how can I remember all this stuff when the snake thing happened, I had to be no more than two years old other things happened too some good and some bad some I don't mind remembering and some I want to forget.

Most kids that live on a farm or in the country have some kind of pet I had a pig, a cute little guy, black and white. I love that pig and my parents gave him to me when he was a small baby, I took that pig everywhere I went. Eventually he got big and then my parents were talking about having him for dinner, that's not right I said that's my little pig, but the little pig had grown up from 8 pounds to 250 but I didn't see him that way. My uncle had a 22 rifle one shot, and I watch him shoot my pig in the head that was devastating to me, but it didn't stop me from chowing down on the ribs and bacon. That taught me to never get too close to my pets you never know whether you'll be having them for dinner or not.

We also used to get chickens in a crate they came in about 50 at the time we ate chickens a lot, but I never got close to one of them. I did have a cat I remembered, she was black and white and when we left the country, we had to leave her behind the cat's name was Sadie. For some reason I still remember Sadie, me and some of the guys putting a fish on a clothesline and letting Sadie jump for it sometimes she could grab it If we didn't put it too high so we put it low enough so she could, that was a good cat. But she stayed from underneath the house and we know why.

The school I was in was one building and had one classroom with a number of grades in it I was in the lower class near the window there was a time during the summer when the windows were open and there were some pear trees or Apple trees, I don't remember which, but they were ripe and hanging from the limb to the ground. I thought in my mind that I would like one of those fruits and really didn't think of the consequences to getting one. So, I looked at those fruits and my mouth started watering and eventually I jumped out the window. Now remember the classroom was full of kids and everyone saw this including the teacher and screamed at me, but I heard nothing and the only thing I saw was the fruits and I picked up two or three and headed back for that same window climb through an offered up a couple to the kids. at that time, the teachers were swatting your hand with a ruler if you did bad but, in my case, they took a paddle and paddle my behind a number of times I never have forgotten that.   End

Everybody's gone.

I used to travel to the big city on a train alone my grandmother used to pin the ticket on my shirt and when I was asleep the conductor would pass by and stamp it with his gadget, he would never wake me up. When I got to the city my grandmother used to always tell me to follow the crowd and that will take me up into the station to my mother who I was meeting. I would spend a couple weeks with my mother and head back to the country to my grandparents and that's the way it went for a couple of years until we all move to the big city Permanently, I think that was the worst move of my life nothing was ever the same after that.

I got in more devilment (that's the way the old people used to say it) then you would believe, and I was still at an early age. I used to hang around with a gang of guys we used to call it a social club, but it was really a gang to make a Long story short I woke up one morning and found all the guys were gone. Among all of them I was the youngest one by 3 to 4 years and I wanted to know where everyone left too. Come to find out everyone had joined the military and naturally I wanted to follow but because of my age I had no chance. The only thing that was different between me and the guys was age, size wise I was just as large as they were. After a number of times trying to get in one service or another, I eventually made it but then that's another story.

End

Thug life

The definition of a thug is a violent person especially a criminal, a member of a religious organization of robbers an assassin in India. Devotees of the goddess Kali, the thugs waylaid and strangled there victims usually travelers, in a ritually prescribed manner. So, the internet says. Is that what you really want?

If you ask kids at an early age the things you see them doing are thuggish, it'll just leave you to believe that's what they want to be. And if you follow their life as they grew up that's what it's leading to. The first thing one of them want is a gun, whether it be water pistols, cap guns, or other until sooner or later it ends up being real and instead of playing cops and robbers they're going into stores and putting there, what used to be play guns in the attendants face at that point it Ceases to be kids playing a game, it begins to get serious.

one time behind bars would be enough for a smart kid but a dump one would go in and out of jail unless he spends a large amount of time the first time, nothing will help him unless he gets in with the hardcore thugs and he really learns to be thuggish then. Is there no way to turn them round, sometimes it will work most times it won't they just have to do the time?

Hopefully, they won't be too old when they get out that they haven't learn anything on the other hand who knows.

One thing is for sure if they spend too much time in there when they do get out thangs will be have changed, their Mama may not be there their Papa and girlfriend for sure, and most of their other relatives may be gone too. it will be a brand-new world and you would have missed out on most of it. Thug life is no life for a young man that wants to see the world no life for a young man that haven't seen anything.

Believe it or not most people don't think about you when you're in the joint, well maybe that's not all true. yo Mama will think about you and maybe your dad. yo girlfriend, no way.

When I'm at the restaurant eating a steak with mashed potatoes there is no way I'm thinking about you until after I eat and maybe not then it's not that you're not on my mind sometime just not all the time. Sometimes I come across a movie with guys been incarcerated and I think about you but really that's about the only time. I also think that a young man needs a young woman it's just natural and not another young man. How would you go, do you live not having a young woman even the touch it's just not normal? Maybe once you get older it would be different but even then, you think about it, you damn sure dream about it sometimes a person has been known to fall out of bed reaching for that someone and fine there's no one there only the floor that you wind up kissing. You look around to see if anyone saw you fall out the bed it's not funny. You get back in the bed and put your pillow where that someone should be and look at your calendar to see how much time you still have left. No one will thank the less of you if you shed a few tears Everyone has done it at one time or another (That's what you tell yourself). You can't go back to sleep so you put your hands behind your head and look around yourself, three other guys in the cell with you how are you going to spend all this time living with this many guys in these close quarters, it can't be done. Then Charlotte comes to mine and Janice and Rose and Bernadette. Oh yeah, there was a lot of girls at that time and I just misuse them. When I did come here one of the girls whispered in my ear, you goanna regret the time you throw me to the wind for Theo's other girls and you know what, she was right. I can't get a card or a letter from them now, none of them. Hell, it's only been he looked at the calendar again; I don't want to even think about it.

End

Trump,

Now that trump has gone, I know that everyone feels a lot better I know I do. We dodged a bullet there for a while I could just imagine what another four years would be like with him in office, him, and his family. You have to admit that he took us through some changes there for a while and he had just started, I do believe the old boy wanted that job forever, another dictator he sure wanted to be another Putin another little Kim another mob boss. Yeah, he would be ready for all that but there's always something that puts a niche into what you want to do what's meant is meant for you maybe that's why you be taken that last ride on Air Force One, have a good trip.

You can keep the people sleep for a while and then they'll come awake and then it's like I know you now and you got to go did you ever realize this; I think not. A man like you as bad as he wants to keep that job what do most anything as you did up to the last. If you wanted to go down in history you made it, there have never been a president like you Ann I would go out on a limb to say there never will be in my lifetime. where will you go now who will be your friend who will want you, the name Trump will forever go down in history to be a Pereira is that what you wanted? You got it.

I heard it would have been better if you wouldn't have ran for president at all you would have Been left with more businesses, banks, golf course and money you would have had it all Except I believe the power That's what was lacking for you. But there nothing like going up and falling back down the second term that would have been a plus for you, but I believe you wanted that second term plus the third an IV just as long as you could beat Obama. You know you still didn't get that Noble Peace Prize Obama received. Oh well, maybe next time. I have a question I wanted to know what you did with that birth certificate? You know Obama's birth certificate that you wanted so bad. But you can say you did beat Obama at one thing and that's the 2 impeachments that you manage to acquire, Trump 2, Obama 0.

And then there came January 20th, 2021 two good things happen that day. Joe Biden was elected president and Donald Trump left the presidency. Two good things happen for America we need to be more aware of who we elected in the future and the enablers they turn out to be worse, I think. If I were not godly, I would wish a large storm would hit Mar-a- Lago (Trump's home) but I would not wish that on anyone not even an ex-president, Would I?

I remember when my Mama died one of my cousins told me, now you the grandpa, I thought for a moment and then I said to myself, but I don't want to be a grandpa It's funny the things you think of when you are alone. My mind be everywhere from the time I was a kid till now, 80 years old, what's up with that.

I wonder if others can remember things like I do it seems kind of odd to me there are things I don't care to remember but I remember them anyway, No I don't like that but there's nothing I can do about it. The good times I always love those the best, bad times not so much. Sometimes I ask the Lord to take those bad times away from me, but he seems to be saying to me that the good times is not worth a dime without the bad and I can understand that I just don't like it. Kind of like if you gamble and you winning all the time you really don't know how it feel if you never lose or something like that.

My life has been full of stories but when you think about it you have to live long enough to get the stories, I guess I'm just about their maybe one day I'll make it before I die that is. Is there anything I've forgotten after over 30 books and three memoirs I don't think so it's getting harder to remember but maybe that's the Alzheimer I could be getting but when I thank, I'm losing it something would pop up that I would remember that I had forgotten and then there it goes again back to that incident or occasion that put me right back to where I was at that time has it ever been that way for you?

Now where would my mind take me this time? What's in the back of my mind that I have forgotten after all these years it's funny when I do remember those things it's like it happened yesterday.

The snow and cold in Alaska, the heat and monsoon in Vietnam, the mama-son's in Korea, and the times they change the money, they changed the money or the strip maybe once or twice a year so the Koreans would not make a killing. They dealt in strip in Korea we called it funny money but when we needed something from the Koreans, we would pay them in script. once a year they would bring it to the base and exchange this money for new money so it would work this way like in the states, they would change the money so that they counterfeiters couldn't get ahold of it; works the same way in Korea but they can only have so much money if they had more than that too bad, they just lost it. Sometimes if a GI were lucky enough to be in town and the villagers knew of the money exchange then they would give that extra money to the GI's and make a deal with them to exchange the money for them and they would split with them, sometimes the GI's would bring the money back and live up to the deal and sometimes they wouldn't. think about it no one knew when the exchange was taking place on the other hand there was always some who did and if one Korean knew the rest knew. The GI's were never worried about being reported because the Koreans wasn't supposed to have the money in the first place. There was a lot of people made a lot of money doing those times and also a lot of people loss a lot of money it was my luck to neither win nor lose. There was a lot of money around, but I wasn't after the money I was after the ladies. They say you can't have both I've heard that, so you have to have one or the other That's the reason I stayed broke all the time, no money but plenty love.

End

Deborah

she was a little bit of everything, a prostitute, a drug dealer, a low life, and a lot more. And she knew those streets she had a good teacher her mother. She always told her if she was goanna be whatever be a good one there's always something in being good at whatever you do, of course no one told her anything about being a nymphomaniac, she believes that came by Naturally. She started by Selling herself graduated up to selling drugs and then selling other girls now she's the Madam. Whenever the men or women came for sex, they always needed some type of pick me up when they were there, she satisfied their needs until one day a fellow came around and she fell for him shouldn't have happened but there it was. He would always come over for one of the other girls and when she wasn't there, he picked her after he found out she was a ****** he came to her more and more then somebody got jealous it was her. She didn't want to see the guy with anyone else even when she was making money off him. She got to the point where she broke into the room they were in and started stabbing on him and her that was a job trying to mellow that out. Then she started going from guy to guy and not charging that was no good for business and eventually she lost her business, and she was out in the street. After that she was given it away when she had no drugs to deal with then she met a girl who she fell in love with the girl came back from work one day and found her with another girl. she started stabbing Debra and the other girl she ended up spending two months in the hospital once she got out, she went back to those same alley's and start doing the same old thing and then she met her mother, now both of them were in the alley doing the same old thing until they were both killed during a threesome.

End

Dear Ire's,

I know you're surprised to hear from me, but I've been meaning to write you for some time now and explain why I left I don't quite understand it myself but at the time I just had to leave maybe one day you'll understand where I'm coming from. You wanted the home life, and I did too up to a point I love the going to work and coming home and go on to dinner sometimes at night and coming back and we making love but then I needed more and then you wanted a baby, that was a little much for me after all I was only 23 and I felt that I had a lot of living to do and really you were holding me back. You kept going on and on about won't know baby, saying all your friends or pregnant and you felt left out I didn't feel that way there was a choice to be made and I had to make it. After some months of you talking about baby, baby I couldn't take it anymore, so I decided to leave. I guess I could have done it a different way maybe even sat down and talk to you about it, but I felt I had over and over, and you just wouldn't have any of it, so instead of just going through all that I packed my bags and left for places unknown. It's been over a year now and I've been thinking about it not about go on back but to explain my situation and hope you'll understand. One thing is for sure I'll never be coming back, and I hate to say that. Ire's you are a good woman and I still love you but I'm just not ready for what you want, maybe one day I'll be kicking myself in the behind and wishing things were different and I had made a mistake but that's the way life is isn't it, you do something an find out years later it was a mistake or wasn't. I hope you're happy an realize that it was better all-around for both of us you may have thought at the time that I made a big mistake an now you may be happy that I left I hope so anyway. I hope you got your child and now you're with the rest of your crew, hell, you may have a couple of kids by now you and the girls can see who's out doing who. Sometimes I feel like I'm sorry I left but that only lasts for a minute then I get over it I hope it's the same for you. Don't get me wrong Ire's I still love you and always will, but I just had to go, I just had to let you know so I'm writing this letter you don't have to write back because I don't know where I'll be anyway, somewhere in this round world I hope, and there's no sense in me saying maybe we'll meet again I'm sure that won't happen. I can see you and me meeting up and you cursing me out (smile). Could happen!

I hope this letter explains somewhat why I left and hope you'll forgive me things don't always go as we want but we'll never know how thangs workout until later in life I hope it works out well for you and for myself, good luck.

Your ex

George

Dear George,

I'm writing this letter even though I know you won't receive it and I have no place to send it to, but I just had to reply even though I'm writing to myself let me just say this:

If you would have sit down and talk to me, I'm sure we could have worked things out, sure I wanted a baby most women do but it didn't have to be right then we could have waited a few years. I love the things you love you have to admit that while you were working, I was working to, did you forget that. I also love making love and going out to dinner at night, but you can't go out to dinner every night although you can make Love every night but I'm really not that good and you weren't either. I miss you and I was surprise to find your clothes plus luggage gone when I got home from work, I must say no one sneaks out the house like that I thought you were a man, Did I intimidate you that much?

George, I love you too and always will, but everything comes to an end even my loving you and I feel one day it'll reach that time but I'm not there yet. I must say though if you were to walk through that door right now that I wouldn't take you back, I guess I'm just weak like that, I've always been weak for you. Maybe we will meet again I hope so and I may curse you out it's possible. But then I think I'll love you and that's for sure, that I know will be true. George, I miss you and I wish you were here right now I wish you would come back I'm sure we could work things out, but things happen and if you don't come back, I'm sure I'll find someone else and I'll love him just as much as I love you and that's for sure. You are right about one thing George, I am a good woman and you missed out, I hope you don't live to regret it.

Love you always.

Ire's.

Take me there

Malcolm, Malcolm that was about the third time she had called me I knew what she wanted but I thought I just play ignorant.

Malcolm, she said again, come here. Malaya was laying in the bed with a sheer nightgown on she likes those sheer things like that.

Now you would think that if you hear a woman call you that many times and you never answered you would think right off the bat that she wants you to come to bed have sex. Well, my woman is not like that she wants something special from me and she get her rocks off when she gets it.

I walked over to the bed and sit down, and she says Malcolm (Take me There).

Look every time it's bedtime you want me to do this don't you think I'm getting tired of it?

Not every time Malcolm.

Just once more Malcolm and I won't ask you again, go over to the bar and get you a large Scotch and water an come back to bed you don't even have to undress.

I said my woman was different she is a little different than other women besides being rich she was beautiful, but she was freaky.

I started telling her the story, she had gotten herself onto two pillows and just watched me and I began.

John and Libby:

Is that what we're going to call them Malaya said.

Are you gonna let me tell the story or are you gonna tell the story which is it going to be?

Tell the story Malaya said.

John and Libby were in the cabin somewhere in the Alaskan mountains, they had been there over three months and they really was getting on each other's nerves.

You wanna screw John said?

Hell, no I don't want to screw Libby said. That's all we do.

I know you bored what else can we do? John said.

Well not that Libby said.

Well, what about some old spades? John said.

Hell no, I don't want that either Libby said.

 Well, I don't know what you wanna do I'm lost.

You always lost, you were lost when we first met, two years later and you still lost.

 I let you talk me into Robing a damn bank and like a fool I went alone with you. Now I'm in the mountains Of Alaska hiding from the law, don't know what the hell I'm doing here the sex is not even that good no more, plenty of men had better than you. Do you hear me John?

I hear this, if you don't stop with the chops, I'm going to take them out for you. Can you understand that? Then all you'd have to do is take care of your wounds. What you need to do is open that bag and look at all that money.

You can't do a damn thing with it up here Libby said. there is not a store within 100 miles of here, damn there's not another house within 10 miles of here what am I talking about.

You can stop talking now Libby I've heard enough.

Well, you can just get the hell outta here, go for a walk or something. Libby said. It's only 20% out there.

You ain't said nothing but the word I'm out of here.

******

John put on his parka other warm attire and left for what he thought was a short stroll and Libby told him good riddance and take his time getting back.

Libby got her a bottle of gin and poured a short one, talking to herself said. I hope he take his time getting back he's getting on my last nerve. There were a few books in the cabin, and she picked up one not caring what it was and started reading.

It had started to snow heavily, and John had lost his way he tried looking at the Sky and the stars but there were none he tried one way for a while and then tried another. Somewhere along the way he ran into a bear family and they started chasing him, he really got lost then. At some point they stop chasing him because they had ran into a deer carcass and he was glad for that but then he was really lost. It started snowing harder and it seemed to him that there was a storm coming along with the snow plus it seemed to him as though it was getting colder. What the hell was he going to do now?

After a couple of hours Libby got to worrying about John and where he was, she would wait a little while longer and go out looking for him although she didn't know the area, she was afraid she might get lost, after all they did still have wild animals out there. She had her a couple more drinks and put on her Parker and other cloths for the element, she would only go out so far once she got lost there was no one to rescue her.

Libby searches further than she intended to even past a bear family that was eating on a deer carcass, she stayed extra wide of them and kept on looking at one point she turned around going back to the cabin but got turn around she felt she was really in trouble then. she started calling out for John but got no answer. Eventually she found a bear den and climbed into it by this time there was a full-blown storm.

Meanwhile John had found a Cave but all it did was to cut down on the wind it was still cold, and he knew nothing about building a fire. that shows you what happens when a city boy meets country. So, he got back as far as he could in The Cave and hope no animals came in wanting to share.

That year was the worse winner Alaska had in 50 years and it was taken no prisoners if you didn't find shelter you were one dead duck.

At that moment, Malcolm looked over at Malaya and saw she was fast asleep and said to his self, it happens every time she never stayed awake for the end of his stories although he never knew the ending his self it was all made up. The only thing he was good at; he finishes his drink cut the light out and went downstairs to read a book.

End

I'll never come this way again.

There are times when you run into a place and say this is the one this is where I'll spend the rest of my life. The streets online with large trees overlapping each other not many automobiles around quite a few old people and young people walking down the street holding hands young kids riding their bikes. The town looking like Mayberry USA, seems like the place to be. I saw all this while looking from the train and decided to get off right then almost left my bags. There was a hotel near an I got me a room overlooking the main street.

I could see the whole town looking from that window, Barber shop, hardware store, market, beauty shop, meat market. Everything right there. I thought I saw a church in there somewhere maybe 2. Yes, this was the place to be I think a little later on I'll go for a walk I think I did see a park at the other end of the street. That's funny I never seen a liquor store and that was alright with me being an X alcoholic.

The place I just left there was a liquor store on each and every block plus you couldn't walk down the street with your grandma in lieu of getting both of you shot my X hometown was no place you wanted to be. Little kids getting shot while there sleeping, cops getting shot in their squad cars. It's not supposed to be like that people are supposed to live out their life without someone else telling them where to go and what to do. I never knew they had places like this maybe I should get around more. The only places I've heard about this is in a story On TV or a book I've read I don't even think they write books about these places anymore, maybe I'll write one and call it home at last, thank God almighty I'm home at last. When I left my home there was no one left mother and daddy both gone other relatives acting an ass and they don't want to leave anyway, my girlfriend had been there forever like me she'll die there like the others don't get me wrong I asked her to come with me, but she says the world is flat there is nothing else outside of this town. After asking her a few times I knew there was no help for her, and I packed my one bag empty my bank account and boarded a train South. I told the conductor to give me a ticket and let me know when it runs out and that's where I'll be. Lucky for me I saw this little town before my money ran out and this will do for me. I don't need much in life just a place where I don't need to duck and hide every night and be able to go on a stroll or two. Maybe take my girlfriend to the park without worrying about stepping on someone's toes and they getting an attitude. And cops not looking at you like you just stole something and then wanting you to run, haven't got there kill quota for the month. Matter of fact I haven't even seen a cop that could be good and could be bad after all if you get in trouble who you gonna call? But then I've only been here a few hours I'll have to find out about that myself. Looking out the window we all look for someone that looks like us I haven't seen anyone that looks like me but on the other hand no one has been looking at me strange and that's the first thing they do when you're new in town.

Looking out the window for a time I realize it was supper time and my stomach started talking to me so I decided to try out the local diner and see what kind of rejections I would get from there. Being a black man you worry about those things, even though you been to war fighting for someone's freedom (surely not mine). And you always have to be on your guard. Sounding naive don't I, well maybe so but that's the way I've survived for all these years and if I keep my wits about me, I'll survive for a little bit longer.

On the way to the diner there were people on the street, and they spoke to me and they were cordial I spoke back the people from my hometown depending on how you look would have moved to the other side of the street when they saw you coming so that was a plus there. I saw a cop on the other side of the street and he just glanced at me no second look. That was a plus. In my hometown they would have stared you down. Another thing was there was only that one police car in my hometown there would have been two or three patrolling the street and if they were to notice me, they may have called for backup. I got to the diner and it had a number of people inside mostly white a few of them glanced at me a waitress came over and asked me where I wanted to sit (plus there). I'm getting plus is all over the place. I ordered a hamburger and fries, a slice of Apple pie and Coke. My order came right on time quicker than I thought it would. Waitress even said can I help you 'Sir' and thank you 'Sir'. I could get to like a place like this, respect that's the word respect. I left the diner and started walking around the first place was the park wasn't big but large enough to have squirrels and a small pond. I even saw a vendor selling peanuts, so I bought a bag and started feeding the squirrels now this was my kind of place. The people in the park were cordial and an old man about my age started talking to me about one thing or another and how long I had been in town. I like the old fellow except that he kind of talk too much. A couple of kids road by on skateboards and they look like they were having their self a ball and that was good in my hometown they would have pulled out a gun and robbed you, the difference in my home and where I am now.

I passed by the hardware store and there was a sign saying help wanted, I walked in and there was an elderly white man behind the counter, and he asked if he could help me? I'm inquiring about the sign you have in the window help wanted I said. Is that job still open?

The sign is still there, and the job is open do you have any experience he said? I have a high school diploma and I'm a fast learner will that do? I'll try you out the white men said.

You can't get any fairer than that I said. When do I start?

Here is an apron he said.

And that's how my first day on the job started that was 20 years ago and now I own the place the town hasn't changed much from the time I got off the train still slow and I like it like that.

End

You never miss your water:

until your well runs dry. Have you ever heard that saying before it really runs true if you think about it? Driving down the street and everything is good until you have a flat and seems like things go downhill from there. After you get your tire fix your air conditioner go out and then your transmission, you thinking about a new car at that time, but you know you can't afford one but anything to stop this from happening. You put your car in the shop and make it home and find the gas is off or electric depending on whether it's summertime or winner if it's winter it's cold as hell in your house or apartment if it's summertime it's so hot in the house you can't handle it same as winter. You find you a hotel and the cost are outrageous, but you have to stay somewhere so you bring out the old credit card and that's close to the limit. As long as it's accepted you don't care, as long as you out the cold or the heat and can take a shower for the moment you all right. But eventually like all things payment come due and you have to lie to the card people, but you don't mind because they're not people anyway there just machines and you have at least 30 days to go before it's due. You go back home thangs seemed to be back to normal , but the rent is do regardless then there's your automobile the payment is due right then bring out the old credit card again, the other one. That's about at the balance too. You need the car to get to your job you need the apartment to lay your head you need the job to pay for it all, a person just can't seem to win.

The cops came to the house on a warrant that I had, took me to jail and told me I could get out on bond, by this time I'm out of money you see it's always about the money. My credit cards were all total out so I couldn't use them my friends I couldn't get ahold of them especially needing money, I never could get ahold of them if I needed a dollar but let me come into money and there everywhere couldn't get rid of them. My girlfriend let's talk about her she's no better than the rest as long as I have money, she good but let me need a few dollars on account then she has to help her mother, right after I come into money, she shows up wanting to go to dinner. Seems like all these people has a nose for when I come into money. It's ironic when I'm doing bad, they never come around but when I'm doing good, I can't seem to get rid of them, when I get home from work there sitting on my doorstep and want to party till the break of day not caring if I have to go to work or not, then come Friday payday there right there. I can't understand it I do believe they have jobs too. Once a couple came over to spend the night because they had gotten Evicted from their apartments, the couple of nights turned into a couple of weeks. The people had to eat but no one volunteered buying any groceries so naturally being a good guy I let that pass they left since that incident and that was more than six months ago (I hear they're doing good now) but I never heard about any reimbursement. Of course, they don't come around anymore.

Once I tried putting a sign on my door saying be back in an hour maybe they would get the message, but they never did, they just sit outside the door some would even go to sleep out there until I got back. There was no back door only one way in an out, so I was stuck I end up opening the door saying I had taken sleeping pills and they just knock me out, I forgot to take the sign down. I think I'm gonna need me some new friends.

I got smart and cut my girlfriend loose whenever she would call, I would always say I was busy or didn't answer the phone at all, it's too bad I had to go that way, but you have to do what you have to do. My expenses I found now are a lot lighter. Paying for one, now I could live with that.

Dates I have a few you have to take one with the other, but you still look for things without having a girlfriend and that's the best route (for me) no one comes into the pad carrying a toothbrush, that's a no no. No one spins the night without leaving 9:00 o'clock that next morning I'm adamant about that. And my phone number is unlisted if I want to see you again, I'll call you.

If it doesn't sound realistic so be it, I'll rough it for a while.

Pretty soon my dates start getting few and far between an I started thinking about my old flame so naturally I gave her a call and you know what she had the nerve to tell me is that she was busy and didn't have time for me and that showed me right there I should have dropped her *** long ago I only started missing her when my well was running dry.

****

We the people / race

They say in the next 50 years you won't even be able to tell one race from the other I was just thinking, the cops that are beating up on one race and the other may be beating up on their own kids

39

somewhere down the road. I don't think these cops see that. They patrolled the streets every day and supposed to be monitoring what's going on but if you think about it, they see but their eyes are not open they may have me as a in law sometime in the future and it's not a damn thing they can do about it, let me explain.

I've got a grandbaby that's white as snow but I'm black as sin, she thinks she's as black as me now figure that one out. You can't tell her any difference she's black like me and that's it. The world is changing, and you have to see it the way it is, there are many Blacks out there that's not into other Blacks changing races and the same with the whites thang about it is there is not a thing we can do about it. Pretty soon we'll be fighting one another and not being able to tell the difference we have a war going on right now. In my lifetime (80) a lot has changed I'm still in awe. when I first went to California you would see it all the time Blacks with white, white with Blacks. When I was in the military and there was a biracial couple, they would make sure that they would send those people to California not the South. Years later when I did go down South and saw a black, white couple I almost had an accident, I had never seen that before. Now when I go down there, I see it all the time an all I can do is shake my head. The world is changing there are those that can see the changes but when you try to tell those that can't see they are amazed.

I remember my uncle telling his kids that he didn't want them marrying a white person I guess he thought he was telling them the right thing, guess what they go out and marry a white person. So now his grandkids are white what can he do about that? The answer is nothing! here I am I never asked for grandkids that are white but here I am, but I find that I don't love them any less they just happened to be kids that are white but knowing in their hearts that they are black, explain that one. Thing is it don't bother the kids at all it's just we old fogies that get upset. Pretty soon with any luck we'll all die off.

Now think about this, who do you think the kids will marry. Before it's over we may have a united nation family.

End

About The Author

Eddie J Martin

Retired US Air Force Sgt.

Books By This Author

Beyond The Curve

Snuggle Puss

Black Russian

www.ingramcontent.com/pod-product-compliance
Lightning Source LLC
Chambersburg PA
CBHW060047150626
46556CB00018BA/3184